To the memory of Harry, Jane, and Larry—
for teaching us that anything is possible.

PUBLISHED BY RIP SQUEAK PRESS
AN IMPRINT OF RIP SQUEAK, INC.
23 SOUTH TASSAJARA DRIVE
SAN LUIS OBISPO, CALIFORNIA 93405

This newly edited and designed edition published in 2005.
Text and illustrations © 2002, 2005 by Rip Squeak, Inc.

RIP SQUEAK®, JESSE & BUNNY™, ABBEY™, EURIPIDES™, and
RIP SQUEAK AND HIS FRIENDS™ are trademarks of Rip Squeak, Inc.

Library of Congress Control Number: 2005926908

ISBN-13: 978-0-9747825-1-5
ISBN-10 0-9747825-1-3
Printed in China by Phoenix Asia
1 3 5 7 9 10 8 6 4 2

New edition edited and designed by Cheshire Studio

Don't miss the other books in this series:
RIP SQUEAK AND HIS FRIENDS *and* THE ADVENTURE

To learn more about Rip Squeak visit
RipSqueak.com

RIP SQUEAK AND FRIENDS
The Treasure

Written by **Susan Yost-Filgate**

Illustrated by **Leonard Filgate**

RIP SQUEAK PRESS ～ SAN LUIS OBISPO, CALIFORNIA

R IP SQUEAK stared out the window, watching an odd-looking figure bouncing toward the cottage. "Jesse, Abbey," he called out. "Euripides is coming. Get ready for another great adventure!" The last few days had been very exciting. First, the humans had packed their bags and left the cottage. Then Rip and his sister, Jesse, had met their new friends, Abbey, the kitten who didn't eat mice, and Euripides, the frog who was a great actor.

Rip heard a *thump* as Euripides came through the cat door, dressed in a new costume.

"What ye starin' at, matey? Never seen a pirate afore? Gather 'round ye landlubbers," Euripides said, hopping onto the bed, dragging a big book behind him.

Rip, Jesse, and Abbey snuggled together and listened as Euripides told
stories about life on the high seas, faraway places, pirates with peg legs
and eye patches, shipwrecks, and buried treasure.

As Euripides finished the last story, a piece of paper fell out of his book.

"What's this?" Euripides wondered.

"Is it a treasure map?" Rip asked excitedly.

"Unfold it!" said Jesse, bouncing up and down.

"It's a map all right!" Rip announced. "And it sure looks familiar—isn't that the pond?"

Abbey looked closely. "I think you're right. What do you think that X means?"

"X marks the spot! I think we have a *real* treasure map," Rip concluded.

"Arghhh," growled Euripides, "an' mebbe it'll lead to some pirate's bounty that we can all share."

"Oh, wow," Jesse exclaimed, her eyes glowing. "A new adventure!"

"First, ye landlubbers," said Euripides, "we must be properly dressed."
He led them to an old trunk where they found colorful scarves, pants, shirts,
and vests—just like the pirates in the book. Soon they were ready to go.

"Wait," said Jesse, as she stuffed something white and red in her pocket.
"What's that?" Rip asked.
"Oh, just something we may need later," she replied mysteriously.

They headed out the door and followed the map to a thicket by the pond. Rip peered into the darkness. "It's pretty scary in there," he said nervously.

"Looks buggy to me," said Abbey, scrunching up her nose.

"Bugs aren't so bad," Euripides replied.

"Easy for you to say," said Abbey, licking her thick fur. "You're a frog."

"Let's go, me hearties!" said Euripides, holding up his walking stick like a sword.
Abbey took a last lick at her fur and said, "One for all and all for one."
Euripides led the way, clearing the path. Rip followed him carrying the map.

As they walked along, Euripides began to sing a song about bugs and creepy crawly things. Soon they were all singing it, even Abbey. Singing always made them feel better.

This thicket's full of creepy things,
with lots of eyes and legs and wings.
But we don't mind, 'cause it's such a pleasure
to work together to find the treasure.

As they moved slowly through the thicket, Rip tripped over the roots of
a tree and the map flew out of his hand.

"Where's the map?" he yelled as everyone began to search.

"There it is!" said Abbey, who was quite good at seeing in the dark.

Rip reached down as far as he could. "Got it!"

When he pulled out the map two ants yelled, "Hey, watch it!" as they tumbled to the ground.

"Sorry," Rip said, startled. "We need our map back."

"Is it a *treasure* map?" asked the tall ant. "Does it lead to a food-kinda-treasure?"

"I don't think so, gentlemen, but you're in luck," said Euripides, pulling two cookies from his pocket.

"Wow!" said the tall ant, taking a bite out of his cookie. "We don't want to be ungrateful, but we've gotta take our treasure and share it with our family."

"Yeah, gotta go!" said the shorter ant as they shuffled off.

When the ants disappeared from sight, Jesse urged everyone on. "Let's go find *our* treasure."

As the adventurers continued on their way they suddenly heard something coming right toward them!

"Duck," yelled Abbey. Everyone fell to the ground.

Then they saw a mother duck with three babies in tow and realized Abbey really meant *duck*.

"Ooohh," the mother duck said. "Are you going to a costume ball?"

"No ma'am," Rip said politely. "We're looking for treasure."

"I have my treasure with me," said mother duck, gently flapping her wings to indicate her children.

"You are fortunate, indeed," said Euripides.

"Well, good luck finding *your* treasure," said the duck, as she and her brood waddled down the path.

"Gee," said Rip, "I suppose a treasure can be something different for each of us."

When they stopped to check the map they heard something buzzing.

"What was that?" asked Abbey. "Did you see that, Rip?"

Before Rip could answer, a strange flying creature hovered above them. His long glowing wings never stopped moving.

Euripides smiled. "I should have known. Sam Aritan, my dragonfly friend."

"Nice treasure map," said Sam, pointing to the X. "I know where that is. Not exactly what I'd call treasure though." Then, as quickly as he had appeared, he vanished into the thicket.

"What did he mean by that?" asked Rip.

"Let's go find out, me hearties!" Euripides shouted. "We're almost there!"

Within minutes, they came to a small clearing
and before them was a most magnificent sight.
  "Wooooow!" they all said in unison.
  "It's just like the one in the book," said Jesse.
  "It's spectacular," added Abbey.
  "Amazing," Euripides remarked.
  "Gee, Sam sure was wrong!" Rip exclaimed.
"This really *is* a treasure!"

Euripides hopped up on to the deck of the ship.

"Come on, mateys," he said with a big smile. "'Tis a perfect day to set sail!"

"Finding this treasure makes me feel like a real pirate," Rip said as he looked around the old ship.

"Finding treasure is what pirates do best," Jesse commented.

"We're as lucky as the mother duck!" Abbey added.

Euripides laughed. "We are lucky, indeed. This ship may not be a treasure to my friend Sam, but it's certainly a treasure to us."

"Every pirate ship needs one of these," Euripides said as he pulled a pirate flag out of his jacket.

"I have a flag, too," said Jesse, holding up the white-and-red cloth that she had hidden in her pocket.

"A heart?" said Euripides. "I've never seen a pirate flag like that."

Jesse looked hurt. "But *our* pirate ship should have a flag that shows we're *good* pirates," she said.

"We're more than just good pirates," Abbey added. "We're a family. A heart says that."

Euripides grinned. "We shall fly both flags. That way we can show who we're pretending to be and who we really are. Prepare to set sail, mateys!"

They hoisted the sails and jumped up and
down on the deck to rock the ship loose.

The old vessel creaked and moaned and a
gentle breeze carried the ship out to open water.

Rip Squeak couldn't wait to find out what
new treasure awaited them on their next
adventure, but then he realized that he already
had the best treasure of all—his wonderful
friends.

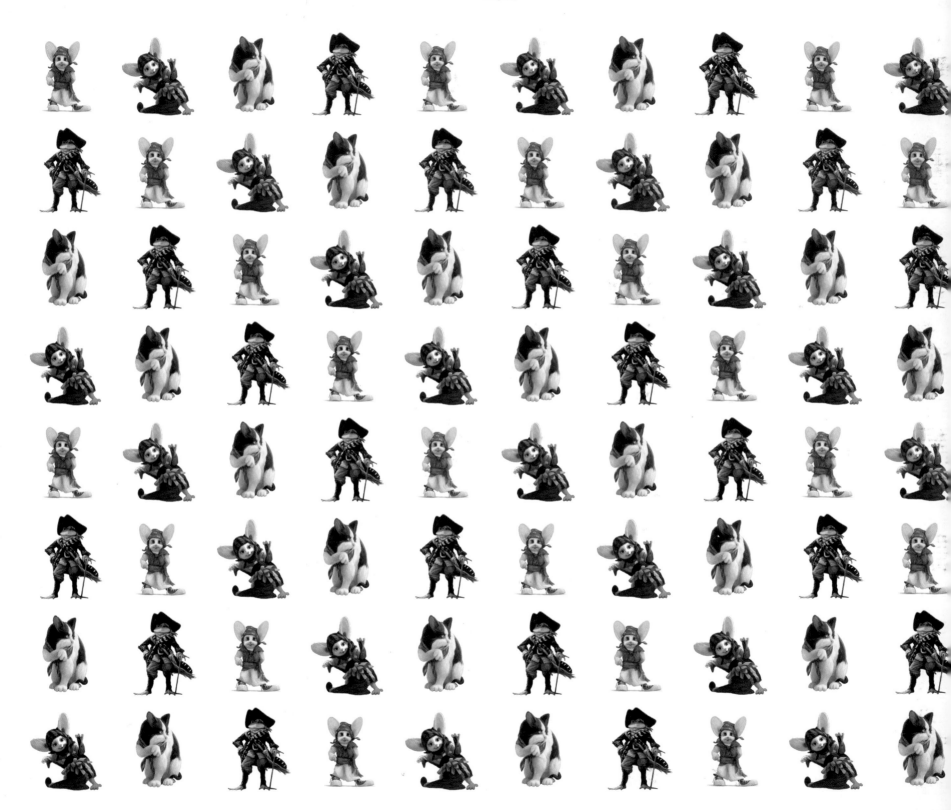